For Leo, who is never tired!

First published in 2017 by Child's Play (International) Ltd
Ashworth Road, Bridgemead, Swindon SN5 7YD, UK

Published in USA by Child's Play Inc
250 Minot Avenue, Auburn, Maine 04210

Distributed in Australia by Child's Play Australia Pty Ltd
Unit 10/20 Narabang Way, Belrose, Sydney, NSW 2085

ISBN 978-1-84643-985-8
CLP260916CPL11169858

Printed in Shenzhen, China

1 3 5 7 9 10 8 6 4 2

A catalogue record of this book
is available from the British Library

www.childs-play.com

MY TAIL'S NOT TIRED!

Jana Novotny Hunter

illustrated by Paula Bowles

"Come on, Little Monster," said Big Monster.
"You must be tired after your busy day."

"No, I'm not," said Little Monster, quick as a wink.
"My knees aren't tired. My knees have lots
of bounces in them."

Big Monster smiled. "SHOW ME!"

So...

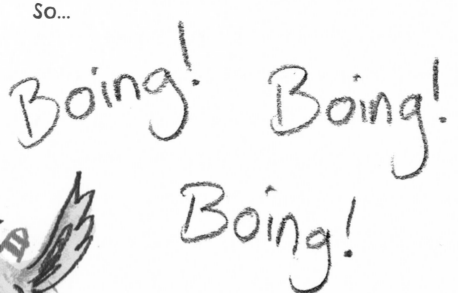

Boing! Boing!

Boing!

...went Little Monster's knees until they had no more bounces left.

Big Monster clapped. "I bet your knees want to rest after that!"

"Yes, but my bottom doesn't want to rest,"
Little Monster replied. "My bottom wants to wiggle-jiggle."

Big Monster nodded. "Of course it does. SHOW ME!"

So...

Wiggle

Wiggle Wiggle

Jiggle

...went Little Monster's bottom until there were no more wiggles left.

"What a fast dance!"
said Big Monster.
"Your bottom must need
to sit down after that."

"Yes, but my tail doesn't need to sit,"
Little Monster insisted.
"My tail needs to swing, swing, swing."

Big Monster groaned.

"SHOW ME!"

So...

Whee!

Whee!

Whee!

...went Little Monster's tail
until it had no more swings left.

"That tail must be
getting sleepy by now,"
suggested Big Monster.

"Maybe a tiny bit.
But my back won't lie still.
It has to roly-poly around."

"All right then. SHOW ME!"

...went Little Monster
until there were
no more rolls left.

"Spectacular rolling!" Big Monster said.
"That tired back must need rubbing."
And Big Monster rubbed Little Monster's
back over and over again.

Aaah!

"Was that a yawn?" Big Monster wondered.

"No!" growled Little Monster.
"My voice isn't tired yet."

"Really? You'd better SHOW ME!"

RAAH!

RAAH!

RAHH!

...roared Little Monster.

"Oh," Big Monster cried.
"What a scary monster!"

"It's only me!
Just your
Little Monster."

"So it is. Your voice must need a rest after all that roaring."

"Yes, but my feet aren't tired yet. My feet have jumps inside them."

"SHOW ME!"

Surprise!

Little Monster jumped up
like a jack-in-the-box.
Big Monster was surprised.

"Now THAT has tired me out!"
Big Monster yawned.
"How about you?"

Little Monster
flapped both arms.
"Not my arms.
My arms need to
fly like a jet plane."

Big Monster sighed. "SHOW ME!"

So...

Zoom!

Zoom!

Zoom!

...went Little Monster round
and round the room...

...landing hard on
Big Monster's lap.

"Goodness!" Big Monster gasped.
"Every bit of you must be tired
after all that jetting about."

Little Monster's horns wobbled.

"Yes, but my eyes aren't tired.
My eyes want to open and shut,
open and shut...

...open,

shut...

shut...

shhh..."

"Shhhhhhhhh..."